Hill City Paranormal
&
Wicked Harvest Books
Presents:
Tales From The Beyond
Series One

Woody G. Watts
Jerrod S. Smelker

TALES FROM THE BEYOND – Series One

Copyright © 2012 Woody G. Watts & Jerrod S. Smelker

All rights reserved.

ISBN: 9798646224621

Hill City Paranormal & Wicked Harvest Books
Presents:
Tales From The Beyond
Series One

All Rights Reserved

Copyright © 2020 Woody G. Watts
Copyright © 2020 Jerrod S. Smelker

This book may not be reproduced, transmitted, or stored in whole or in part by any means, including graphic, electronic, or mechanical without the express written consent of the author except in the case of brief quotations embodied in critical articles and reviews.

Author: Woody G. Watts and Jerrod S. Smelker

Editor: Bailey K. Lockwood at Just Ducky Editing

Cover Design: Woody G. Watts

Contact Info:

Hill City Paranormal
www.hillcityparanormal.com
Social Media: @hillcityparanormal
Call Us: 701-HAUNTED
Email: hillcityparanormal@gmail.com

Wicked Harvest Books
www.LastLeafPublishing.com
www.WickedHarvestBooks.com
www.JerrodSmelker.com
Email: jsmelker@hotmail.com
Jerrod S. Smelker, LLC

Acknowledgments and Thank You

Woody G. Watts and Hill City Paranormal would like to thank the following:

DEDICATED TO "LITTLE SHUG"

To my lovely wife, Laura, for loving me and being my best friend in this blessed life.

To my amazing dad Graham, mom Kathy and sister Ashley for always supporting me.

To my neighbor and friend Jeremy for riding along on every adventure.

To the real talent Jerrod for capturing the tone and atmosphere of the stories in my head and THE BEYOND.

Psalm 139:14

I praise you because I am fearfully and wonderfully made; your works are wonderful, I know that full well.

Acknowledgments and Thank You

Jerrod S. Smelker and Wicked Harvest Books would like to thank the following:

To my beautiful wife, Shana, who supported me, tossed ideas my way for story concepts and was as excited as I was about this project. Who always sits through hours and hours of paranormal shows with me because she knows I love them.

To my wonderful kids Jake, Kylan, and Sadrie, who I couldn't be prouder of.

To my parents, always.

To the awesome and gifted Mr. Woody G. Watts, for allowing me the opportunity to be a part of this amazing project. Cheers to you, Laura, and everyone at Hill City Paranormal. I hope for many more projects in the future.

To my outstanding editor Bailey K. Lockwood for fixing... well... everything.

To my niece Katie who loves all things creepy and spooky.

Woody G. Watts was born and raised in Virginia. Having lived in and around the Hill City his whole life he knows the area well. He has had a video camera in his hand since he was 14 years old and has been making sci fi/horror/comedy videos ever since.

He owns and operates a commercial production company, Watts Creative Studios, and often puts Bigfoot, Aliens and Ghosts in his productions.

Woody founded Hill City Paranormal to capture video evidence of the many local legends he's always heard in his hometown. He currently lives in Lynchburg, Virginia with his wife Laura and two dogs, Ellie and Frances.

Jerrod S. Smelker is the owner/operator/writer for Last Leaf Publishing and Wicked Harvest Books. Author of "*Vigilant in Today's World*" series of crime prevention books, "*Wicked Harvest: Michigan Monsters & Macabre*" series of spooky short stories and books along with numerous other short stories. He grew up in Ionia, a quaint small town smack dab in the middle of Michigan between Grand Rapids and the state's capital, Lansing. He enjoys history, writing, reading, fine cigars and pipes, craft beers and hard ciders, bourbon and moonshine, good coffee (with French Vanilla creamer), and Michigan road trips. He is a small town boy at heart whose soul is forever deeply rooted in the fall season and the Halloween holiday. He currently lives in Grand Blanc Michigan with his wife Shana, kids and cats.

TALES FROM THE BEYOND – Series One

CONTENTS

Introduction

The Tree Line   Pg # 1

Into the Fray   Pg #10

Prospecting   Pg #17

Dead Ringer   Pg #26

Voodoo App   Pg #35

Dead Diary   Pg #46

Boys Beware   Pg #54

Soul of Crows   Pg #63

Strawman   Pg #72

Legend Of Virginia Train 403   Pg #83

Welcome to Hill City Paranormal

How and when did you start Hill City Paranormal is a question I get a lot these days. Each time I get asked, I have a different answer.

Hill City Paranormal has always been part of me and the world I live in, even if it didn't yet have a name. When I was 14 years old, I picked up my first video camera and began making films, parodies, and stop motion shorts. I even remember editing projects between two VCRs and then dubbing them with a cassette player. So to say the retro VHS vibes are strong in me is an understatement.

During that time, my family and I would go for long car rides around our town, listening to radio dramas. They would graciously allow me to film ghost hunts or parodies of films we had recently seen. This is where I started to insert my love for all things paranormal and unknown into my "craft".

My father and I would make fake Bigfoot videos and alien attack films. Fast-forward 24 years later, I now own my own video production company and have produced over 1,600 commercials, many of which still include my favorite characters such as Bigfoot, aliens, and ghosts. As you can see, my love for all things paranormal and VHS tracking defects, cassette audio distortion, and filming have been around for a long time.

It wasn't until a few years ago though that I had to officially give it a name, and that name was Hill City Paranormal. My video production company was asked to film and facilitate a Haunted History Tour at our local Academy Center. As you can imagine, I jumped at the opportunity and could not wait to start producing official paranormal content. I knew early on, though, that I didn't want people to mistake this event for a normal "production" and to write it off as a video project. That's when I decided to officially start Hill City Paranormal and produce this show and others to follow. This gave me a chance to connect with tour participants on another level; instead of a behind the scenes production company. So with that, Hill City Paranormal was born, and I began to make it official with a website, merchandise, and videos.

Many of the same people that have been a part of my production company are also a part of HCP. My lovely wife Laura, my go-to skeptic Jeremy, my hysterical father Graham, and the occasional intern (often Todd) all help to make this possible. While we do investigations, we offer what I believe to be a different spin on them. We love to explore, go on adventures, and often rely 100% on video evidence. We lean heavily on the production side that I'm use to instead of other methods that are often out there. That's what I believe separates Hill City Paranormal in such a diverse field that we love.

One of the added bonuses of founding HCP and having a video production company is that whatever we dream up, we can create. That's why you'll see a big mix of actual investigations, fun parody videos, a podcast, and even this wonderful book you're about to read. As a creator, my worlds often merge, and that's exactly what *Tales from the Beyond* is about. While we do actual investigations, we also love Sci-Fi, paranormal and anything cryptid related. Being creators, you can see how often we just want to insert our passions into what we do in our daily lives.

With Hill City Paranormal, you'll get a blend of investigations, entertaining fictional stories, and just plain fun. So as you can see, Hill City Paranormal is so much more than a name to me, it's really my personality and what goes on inside this crazy mind.

TALES FROM THE BEYOND – Series One

Luray Caverns Alien Interview Behind The Scenes

Woody and Laura

THE TREE LINE

The early summer fog blankets the yard just before sunrise in Lynchburg, Virginia. Woody steps out onto his deck to enjoy some quiet time before his wife Laura and their two dogs, Ellie and Frances, awaken. He enjoys many Sunday mornings this way. It's a way for him to relax, decompress from a busy week and reconnect with his thoughts. Woody stretches his arms and yawns and then sits in his favorite Adirondack chair, enjoying his coffee and the serenity of a peaceful morning. His camera is by his side, as it is every morning when he sits on his deck, just in case he has an opportunity to get a perfect shot of a sunrise or a rare bird.

He sips his coffee and lies his head back on the chair, closes his eyes, and listens to the birds and the breeze rustling the leaves. It's calm, peaceful. Just beyond the deck and small back yard is the tree line. His property runs adjacent to a sizable forest. Woody and Laura enjoy hiking and exploring the woods whenever they have the chance. He loves to take photos and videos of nature while exploring. The trees, hills, and scenery are what made them fall in love with the area and their home in the first place. They are far away from other houses, far from the city, and their home is quiet and quaint; the perfect place for them to raise a family.

Woody's morning serenity breaks with a noise coming from the tree line. His eyes dart open and he lifts his head quickly. *Crack!* There it is again, a small branch breaking. He sits up in his chair and looks around, but can't see anything. His heart begins to beat a little faster. He's heard many animals in the woods before, but this sound is slightly different than anything he has ever heard. *Crack!* This time it is even louder, and Woody's body shakes, spilling a bit of his coffee. His eyes widen, and he strains to see what is out there. The sun is just coming up, so it is partially dark, difficult to see.

Woody pulls himself from the chair, leaving his camera and the steaming coffee cup on the armrest. He stares at the tree line, looking for any movement through the low hanging fog and dim light. The hair on his arms stand straight up and a chill runs from his head to his feet. He shuffles a few feet to the deck railing, grasping it and holding on tight with both hands.

"Heeeelllooooo." He reluctantly calls with a slight quiver. Woody hopes no one will actually say anything back to him, but then again, he hopes someone will.

Dead leaves at the tree line begin to make noise. He could hear something walking through the woods, walking toward him. He tries to swallow, but his throat is too dry. His eyes go wide, and his hands begin to shake. It is moving closer. He struggles to look and see it, but there is nothing. Panic overcomes him. He turns from the railing to run back into the house but stops himself. Instead, he grabs his camera and starts taking photos of the tree line. Even overcome with fear, he wants to see what this is.

He pushes the camera's shutter button as fast as he can. The flash goes off over and over, lighting up the entire back yard. Even with the camera in his face and the bright light, he still can't see what was coming toward him. After a dozen or so shots, he heard whatever it was running back into the tree line. He hears the light *thumps* on the ground, leaves crunching, and small branches breaking in its wake. Woody's heart is beating faster, and his hands are trembling. He tries to calm himself down, knowing that whatever this is, it fled into the forest.

Woody sits back in the chair and takes a large gulp of his coffee. Part of him wishes for something much stronger than coffee to calm his nerves. He takes a few deep breaths and starts to rationalize what had just happened.

"A raccoon." He tells himself aloud. "It was probably just a darn raccoon." This time he says it out loud and with the start of a smile. He chuckles at himself, thinking that a simple woodland creature gave him such a scare. He sits back in the chair, smiles, and takes another drink. He laughs, relaxes into his chair, and thinks about telling Laura about how a fuzzy raccoon fouled his peaceful morning.

A few moments pass, his coffee cup is empty, Woody decides to go inside for another cup. As he stands up, he glances down at his camera. He took a few photographs; the flash is likely what scared it away, but... was there anything in the photos?

"Photos of what? A black-masked, fat raccoon?" He

chuckles to himself with a slight grin. He brushes it off and gets himself another cup of coffee.

Woody returned to the deck and watched the sun peek from the horizon from his chair. The fog dissipates, and the air warms by the minute. His eyes roam the back yard, and then the sky, back to the yard and then to the camera sitting next to him. Curiosity now has the better of him. He picks up the camera, turns it on, and start to scan through the last photos.

First picture, nothing. Second picture, nothing. Third picture, nothing.

"Ugh, this is silly." He rolls his eyes at his foolishness.

As he sets the camera down, the fourth picture fills the LED screen. He freezes. He stares at it, then pulls the camera closer to his face. He stares at the photo intently, his face contorting from disappointment to puzzlement. He clicks over to the next picture. Puzzled turns to absolute horror in a split second. He shudders, and his pulse begins to races. He clicks back to the fourth photo, then forward to the fifth, then sixth, and so on. His eyes bulge with each click.

"Oh, my...oh my...an...an...*ALIEN!*" Woody's grip on the camera is so tight the plastic makes a creaking sound. He's excited and terrified at the same time.

Woody has always believed in UFOs and aliens, and even though he thought he had seen a UFO many years before, Woody never thought he would experience anything like this in his lifetime. He paces back and forth on the deck, looking at the photos. A part of him wants to run inside and wake Laura, but the other part of him has other thoughts, different plans. He wants to see them. He wants to know what was in the woods.

The excitement is too much for Woody to ignore, and Woody pushes down the anxiety that filled every inch of his body. He cinches up his robe, slides on his slippers, grabs a flashlight and his camera, and heads to the tree line. His heart was beating fast before; it now feels like it is going to explode from his chest. He tries to calm himself down with each step he took across his back yard but has no luck.

The morning sun is rising rapidly, but the deep woods are still as dark as night. Woody can only see a few feet in front of him, even with the bright flashlight to guide him. His camera sways from his neck with each step further into the foreboding forest. He has no idea in which direction he should be going or how far he is willing to go. A feeling draws him to find the alien, to get more proof that they exist.

Step after step, Woody dodges fallen trees and moss-covered rocks. He tries to tiptoe, but the dead leaves and pine needles make it impossible. Five minutes have gone by when Woody notices a faint orange light through the trees in front of him. He moves closer and closer to where the light gets brighter. As he steps around a large oak tree, he sees it.

A matte black craft, the size of a large delivery van, but resembling a submarine hovers just above the ground. A bright orange light emits from the front and the back of the odd-looking ship. Woody is half-hidden by a tree but can see the craft clearly now, a few feet in front of him. His body tenses, and for a moment, his mind is entirely blank. He's mesmerized by what he sees in his once-familiar forest.

He turns off his flashlight and slowly puts it in his robe pocket. He pulls the camera up to his eye, looks through the viewfinder, and snaps photos. After several photos, the craft starts to rotate slowly. In a panic, Woody lets the camera drop to his chest and takes off toward his home. He's never run so fast in his life.

"Oh, man! Oh, I gotta get on my podcast and tell everyone, but no one is going to believe me. But they have to, right? They *have* to? It's real; I have *proof!*" Woody's breathing is deep, his heart is racing, and his body is tingling all over. He is terrified and exhilarated all at once.

Woody breaks through the tree line only to trip over a low branch. As he falls, he braces the camera to his chest and twists his body to land flat on his back. He groans and closes his eyes as he hits the grass and has the wind knocked out of him. He opens his eyes and tries to take in a breath. He quickly glances down his body to make sure his camera is safe and undamaged. He breathes a deep sigh of relief once he sees that there was no damage done in the mad dash through the woods and begins muttering to himself as he gets to his feet.

"This is big; this is really big. *Huge* even, this is so huge. No one is going to believe me." He brushes pine needles and dirt from his clothes.

He takes a step toward his house, and a bright beam of white light coming from the forest envelopes his entire body. He cannot move. He tries to take a step forward. He tries to raise his arms. Nothing. Trapped.

His heart pounds as fear and adrenaline courses through him. His entire body begins to be pulled backward into the woods by the light.

"No one will believe meeeeeee!"

****

The sun rose and broke above the tips of the trees. Laura slides open the deck door with a hot cup of coffee in her hand. She takes a deep breath smelling the warm summer morning air, smiling as she takes in the beautiful scenery. She hears the birds chirping and a slight breeze rustling the leaves. As she takes a sip from her cup, she looks at the tree line and notices a camera lying in the grass. She looks from left to right and calls out tentatively, "Woody? Woody?"

INTO THE FRAY

As a historian, Jeremy enjoyed visiting the many historical sites that the state of Virginia had to offer. From Colonial Williamsburg to the many civil war battlefields, he appreciated and respected them all. Jeremy, a former Army soldier, was what many would call a skeptic. Especially true when it came to the paranormal. However, that changed one day in the spring of 2019.

On April 9th, 2019, Jeremy visited the historic civil war battlefield in Appomattox, Virginia. It was the 154th anniversary of the battle of Appomattox County Court House. Both the Union and Confederate Army's fought hard, but in the end, the Union prevailed, leaving the Confederates to surrender.

Hundreds of acres of battlefield had been preserved,

and it had many visitors over the years to learn about the civil war and the infamous battles. This was Jeremy's first visit to the location, and he was eager to learn about the history, take a few photos and hopefully find a few antique treasures along the way.

The day was rather warm, full of sunshine with a soft breeze blowing through the large oak trees. It was quite early in the morning when Jeremy arrived. There were only a few people milling about including a few park rangers. Jeremy opted to forgo the offered tour and walked the grounds by himself. He often explored historical sites alone to gather his thoughts and get a real feel for what he was experiencing.

An hour had passed, and Jeremy found himself walking up a high ridge. The grass was knee-high, swaying back and forth like waves of a green ocean. He stopped at the top, mesmerized by the cool breeze shifting and bending the grass. He took a step forward and felt something at his feet. He looked down and spotted something black and brown. He got down on one knee to get a better look.

He pushed the grass away with each hand and noticed the object sticking up out of the ground. It was long, and made of metal and wood. He gripped it and pulled it from the dirt toward his chest. He looked it up and down, brushing the earth from it. A smile stretched over his face. *Unbelievable*, he had found an authentic civil war rifle. He wiped more dirt and grime off of the metal and read "Springfield" stamped into it. He stared, inspecting every detail of it.

Jeremy was about to stand up to get his newfound prize into the sunlight for a better look. He gripped the rifle tight but felt light-headed. Stumbling slightly, Jeremy slowly knelt to the ground. He took a few deep breaths and blinked a few times, trying to get his bearings.

"Must be the hot sun." He said to himself aloud.

He tried again to stand but failed. He felt fatigued. Sweat dripped down his forehead, down the bridge of his nose, and over his cheeks. His heart pounded. He began to hear faint sounds of what sounded like gunshots and yelling. He looked across the grass but saw nothing. He blinked his eyes a few times before he blacked out.

"Fire it, soldier!! Fire your weapon!" A Union lieutenant grabbed Jeremy's shoulder, screaming in his ear.

"Get in the fight, soldier! Fire that weapon!" He screamed again as he picked Jeremy up from his knees.

Jeremy was frozen, confused, looking around at the scene surrounding him. His head spun as the lieutenant pulled him to his feet.

"What is going on?" Jeremy asked aloud, whipping his head around from one side to the other.

"Who are you? Where am I?" He looked at the lieutenant next to him. The lieutenant ignored the questions and kept yelling commands to him and the others around them.

As Jeremy stood there, overwhelmed by the smells of gun powder and the scent of death, his face turned pale, and his stomach felt tied in knots. In that instant, he came to the horrifying realization...he was a Union soldier back in 1865 on the deadly battlefield of Appomattox Court House.

Lead Minié balls were flying through the air from every direction. Jeremy could hear them whizzing past, whistling and hard thumps as they hit soldiers to his right and left. Blood spattered on his left side where a soldier had just been standing next to him. He turned his sights forward to see the nightmare before him. Hundreds of Confederate soldiers were charging up the ridge towards him.

Smoke choked his lungs as the lieutenant looked back at him and again screamed for him to shoot. He looked down at his hands. He was holding the Springfield rifle, now in pristine condition. Still confused and terrified, he brought the butt of the rifle to his shoulder and, without even aiming, pulled the trigger. The rifle roared, punching his shoulder back, blocking his vision with smoke.

The Confederates ran, gaining ground faster than the Union soldiers could back up the ridge. Many soldiers from both sides were now resorting to using their rifles as clubs or stabbing with bayonets. Jeremy turned to run up the hill when he felt the bottom right side of his coat blow out. He looked down to see a bullet had ripped through, luckily missing his body by an inch. He screamed and dashed forward with a new life-preserving fervor.

He struggled to run, tripping over dozens of dead Union comrades and dodging cannonball blasts. As he reached the crest of the hill, he could see auxiliary soldiers coming from the other side of the ridge. They were passing him quickly, heading straight for the Confederates with Old Glory leading the way.

Jeremy quickly reloaded his Springfield and turned to make his way down the ridge toward the enemy. If he was in this fight, then by God, he was going to fight. He stopped after a few steps, raised the rifle and pulled the trigger. Before the shot left the barrel, a cannonball exploded directly in front of him. Grass and dirt launched into the air. The blast took Jeremy off of his feet, tossing him back and to the ground. He blacked out.

Jeremy opened his eyes. He was lying on the ground, looking up at the April 9th, 2019 sky. The sun was blinding him as he squinted to see. There were no sounds except for the breeze through the tall grass and chirping birds. He laid there for a few minutes, not moving an inch. Puzzled, he listened for gunshots and yelling. He sniffed the air for gun powder or smoke. There was nothing.

He shook his head, and the skeptic that he was, started to laugh.

"A dream. HA! I must have passed out from the heat

and had a bad dream." He continued to chuckle and lifted his head.

"Wow, what a crazy dream." He sat up and rubbed his eyes. Then he looked down over his body.

Disbelief and bewilderment surged through his entire body and mind. He saw the pristine Springfield lying in the grass to the right of him and that his body was adorned with a complete Union soldier uniform. With a bullet hole in the right side of the dark blue sack-coat.

Jeremy stuck his finger through the tattered hole. "Wait. What just happened?" He shook and yelled out for help.

PROSPECTING

Thump! Thump! Thump!

"Oh my God, what is that?" Beth whispered. Her body wide awake and shaking.

"Shhhhhh!" Ted sat up in the tent, trying to listen to the sounds.

"What is that?" Beth grabbed ahold of Ted's arm and leaned in closer to him. She tried to whisper quieter, but her voice was actually louder.

"Quiet, I don't know." Ted attempted to get his point across to stop talking by whispering in a tone of authority. Beth had heard this tone before, and she ignored it just like she had every other time.

Thump! Thump!

"Oh God, Ted, its right outside the tent." She pulled on Ted's arm, squeezing it hard enough to send pain through his arm.

"Ouch! Please, Beth, be quiet." He grabbed ahold of her hand and tried to pry her fingers loose. Her nails dug deeper and deeper into his flannel shirt.

"We can hear you in there, guys. It's just us; Graham and Kathy."

Ted, with full adrenaline dump taking over his body, unzipped the tent door fiercely. He was relieved as well as annoyed. He stormed out of the tent, leaving Beth behind. She struggled to remove herself from the zipped sleeping bag, then finally freeing herself, clambered out as well.

"Graham! What are you guys doing? You gave us a heart attack." Ted wiped his eyes and looked up at the night sky. It was a clear, star-filled sky with a bright half-moon. He walked a few steps, making sure not to fall in the fire pit still full of burning embers.

"Well, what did you think it was? A bear? A mountain lion? Bigfoot, perhaps?" Graham knelt down, rummaging through the cooler for a drink and handing a few snacks to Kathy. His back was to Ted and Beth.

"Funny, Graham...but yeah, it could have been any of those things." Ted joined Graham at the cooler. They each grabbed a cold soda. Beth stood at the tent door, watching the boys. She shook her head and rolled her eyes at Kathy before she went back into the tent.

Graham was about to enter his tent with Kathy. "HA!! Bigfoot? Really? Come on. There's no such thing, and you know it."

The summer of 2019 in Bear Creek, Virginia was unexpectedly hot. Graham, Kathy, Ted, and Beth had been camping throughout the state together when they had the time, sometimes in campgrounds, sometimes in the middle of nowhere. Graham had a passion for gold prospecting, and he dragged Kathy along with him every chance he could. And every so often, they would drag another couple along with them. Every campsite had to have a river, stream, or creek to pan for the shiny treasure. Graham had done fairly well, always finding a small nugget or two on every trip.

Graham, now in his late 50's, had been prospecting in the Bear Creek area for years. He had come into contact with many animals and people. All of his adventures were relatively tame. He had heard stories about hikers and campers disappearing his whole life but chalked it up to them being inexperienced. He scoffed at stories of UFOs, Sasquatch, and anything paranormal.

The two couples woke the next morning, shared breakfast and coffee, and then Ted, Beth, and Kathy went hiking while Graham retrieved his prospecting tools and headed for the creek. The sun was up, and the heat was already making Graham sweat. His mind wasn't on the weather though, just finding gold.

Graham found a quiet secluded spot at the creek bed. The creek was shallow in the area, only a foot or so deep with crystal clear water that was cool to the touch. To the west was an open grassy area with a few pine and maple trees dotting the landscape. To the east was a smaller grassy area and then a vast forest that went on for miles.

He removed his backpack, spilling the contents onto the grass. Out poured his water bottles, a few snacks, a small shovel, dowsing rods, and his lucky prospecting pan. The pan wasn't much to look at, a simple metal camping pan that once had blue paint, but was chipped and rubbed off years ago. He loved it because it had presented him with gold more times than not.

A smile stretched across his face as he worked the dowsing rods to help pinpoint the best location for panning. Once he found a good spot, he got down to business. He would dig into the creek bed and fill the pan with dirt and stones. He let the water swish back and forth while tossing the larger rocks. His eyes were keen when it came to spotting anything shiny.

Graham continued shuffling his pan back and forth, tossing the larger stones and rocks aside. He moved his head to one side, letting the full rays of sunshine reach the pan. He moved his finger back and forth through the sand left in the pan, hoping to see the sunshine back at him in the form of gold morsels. Nothing. He tossed what remained from the pan to the side of the creek and scooped again. Nothing.

Hours had passed and it was the same; no sign of gold. Graham told himself that he'd give it another ten minutes, then pack up to head for camp. He placed the pan in the water, scooped up the sand and rock, and began to separate. He cocked his head to the side, letting the sunshine take over the pan again.

As he was removing a larger stone, something in the pan seemed to sparkle. He paused and looked closer. He dumped some of the water and moved a few sand particles to the left. To his delight was a small piece of gold. A broad smile covered his face as he dug the chunk out. He held it on his wet fingertip, letting it glisten in the sunlight.

The world around Graham seemed to disappear as he gazed at his new-found wealth, albeit a small amount, he was still jubilant about his discovery. He was about to place the nugget in his shirt pocket when the sun's rays were suddenly blocked by something behind him. He could see the shadow overtake his own along with the creek bed.

"Hey, Kathy, I found one!" Graham smiled as he turned to greet his wife and show her his new prized possession.

What was standing behind Graham was not his wife. It was not Ted or Beth. It was not a human at all. Towering over him was a colossal beast. Graham was eye level to the beast's lower chest. He strained and lifted his head to match eyes. Eyes that were black as the night.

"Bi...Bi...BIGFOOT!!!" Graham screamed, barely getting the word out.

The beast let out the most terrifying guttural howl

shaking Graham to his core. He tried to run, but he was frozen in fear. The creature wrapped its arms around Graham, squeezing him tighter than he had ever felt. He couldn't breathe, and he could feel his ribs start to crack. The pain was so intense he blacked out.

Graham woke a few minutes later with the beast grasping his left leg. His head and body were scraping the grass and gravel as he was being pulled across the ground. He could see they were leaving the creek, heading towards the woods. The sun blinded him as he tried to look up at the beast. His heart was pounding. He tried to escape by jerking his leg from the beast's grasp, but it was no use. He began to scream for help as the beast started to enter the dark woods dragging him behind.

"Hey, Graham?" Kathy yelled from the other side of the creek, not able to see her husband even though she thought she had heard him moments before.

"Help! Help!" Graham yelled back, desperately hoping his wife and friends could save him.

Kathy, Beth, and Ted ran towards Graham's pleas for help. They couldn't see him but knew he was just inside the forest.

To Graham's disbelief, the massive hairy creature released its constricted grip from his leg and ascended deeper into the forest. It crashed through the brush and small trees without hesitation. Graham lay on the ground, covered in dirt and dead leaves. He tried to catch his breath as his chest pounded. He got to his feet and limped out of the woods towards his wife's voice.

"Graham! Graham! Are you okay?" Kathy caught Graham who was barely able to stand as he came from the woods into the grassy area. She could clearly see the look of terror on his face.

Ted and Beth finally caught up to the couple. Graham tried to speak, but he could only mutter a few words, making no sense to his wife and friends.

"Geez, Graham, what happened? You're covered in dirt, and your clothes are a mess." Ted circled Graham, looking him over and helping to brush off the debris.

Graham took a large swig of water from his wife's water bottle, much of it running down his face as he struggled to breathe.

"B...B...Bigfoot!" Graham collapsed to the ground, trying to comprehend what had just happened. His body shook.

"Bigfoot?" Ted said sarcastically, shaking his head at his disheveled friend. "There's no such thing as Bigfoot, Graham, you said so yourself."

Graham lifted his left pant leg, revealing a bruise in the shape of a giant handprint.

"Then where did this come from?"

DEAD RINGER

"Hello Laura, I'm Doctor Dana Murphy" The psychiatrist shook hands with Laura, and then took a seat behind a large dark oak desk. She took out a notepad and pen, writing the date and time.

"Hello," Laura barely looked up to make eye contact. She sat across the desk in a chair that she was convinced made her uncomfortable on purpose.

"Do you know why you are here today?" Dr. Murphy looked up from the notepad at Laura and then pulled a file from a bottom drawer.

"Yes."

"Good. Can you tell me about what happened last October?" Dr. Murphy adjusted her bifocal glasses and clicked her pen ready to write.

"You mean at the Western State Lunatic Asylum?" Her tone smug and condescending. She squirmed in the chair, twisting her long blonde hair.

"Well, we like to call it simply the Western State Hospital," Dr. Murphy shifted in her chair, making it creak. A slight grin pulled her face back a little as she was trying to be politically correct.

Laura sat up in the chair and leaned forward, slightly touching her chest to the wooden desk. She looked into the good doctor's eyes, and grinding her teeth, deepened her voice to a more serious and ominous tone. "You can call it whatever you like, but it's a place of pure evil."

Laura sat back in her chair, staring at the tuft of hair she was twisting. She looked at the doctor and then back to her hair. She took a deep breath and began to tell her story.

"Last year, I was a naive 25-year-old nursing student. I was also a hobby paranormal investigator. I followed my husband into some of the craziest places to investigate ghosts and other weird and mysterious things. Some of the places we enjoyed exploring were old abandoned buildings such as jails, prisons, and even asylums... or state hospitals... as you prefer to call them.

"Anyway, we decided one day to conduct an investigation at the Western State Lunatic Asylum over in Staunton. Now, this place was not completely abandoned. In fact, funny enough, after it was a state hospital, it became a prison, then after that closed, they started renovations to turn it into condos. Can you believe that? Condos!" Dr. Murphy's eyebrows rose as she nodded and made a small note.

"When we investigated, only a portion of the property and buildings had been renovated. There were many under construction and a few that hadn't been touched in years. My husband was friends with one of the general contractors, and he gave us full access to the untouched buildings for our investigation.

"I honestly don't remember what building we were in that night. There were so many, and to me, they all looked alike. I can tell you that driving up to the property at night and seeing the foreboding buildings sent chills up my spine and made the hair on my arms stand straight up. I had a bad feeling about that night but did my best to push on." Laura rubbed her arms subconsciously with the memory.

"We only had flashlights, a digital recorder, and a digital camera with us. Our investigation was only going to be an hour or so, so we didn't bother with the other equipment. I was in charge of the digital camera. I was just to take random shots of rooms, hallways, and anything that looked interesting.

"I remember the weather was quite pleasant and warm; however, it had been raining all day. The rain was coming down lightly at times, and then sudden downpours here and there. We met with the general contractor, who gave us the keys. He told us a few things to be careful of; the damaged floors due to rot and all of the ghosts. He said 'ghosts' playfully but told us a few supposedly true stories of malicious things that had happened there." Laura made air quotes with her figures as she said 'true stories'.

"One was of a young nurse who had transferred there back in 1932. Her name was Nancy. She loved her job and was good at it. However, Nancy had a wicked side. Rumor had it she beat and tortured patients daily and laughed about it. Allegations were that she purposely starved people, gave them rotten food, and lock them in their rooms for days. For 15 years, she did this until one night; some of the patients had enough.

"A dozen patients waited for Nancy to come on shift one night. As she donned her white hat, they jumped her and beat her to death with pipes, boards, and even a lamp. She bled to death on the vinyl floor to be found the next morning. Sweet revenge most called it. Legend has it her body was buried on the grounds in an unmarked grave." Dr. Murphy didn't flinch at the grotesque story but met Laura's eyes sharply.

"Then he said something that made me even edgier than I already was. He told us to watch out for the shadow people. When I asked what he had meant by that, he simply said that many people living in the condos and construction workers had seen shadowy figures in the buildings and around the property... and it was never a pleasant experience. He said people think they are the former patients of Nancy's, roaming the night for revenge. He laughed after telling us this, admitting that he was a big skeptic when it came to legends and fables like that.

"He left us to our investigation after that. We gathered our things and walked to a large, abandoned building. Many of the building's windows had been broken out, and the roof was leaking. The smell of mold and mildew permeated the air no matter where you were.

The paint was peeling from the walls, and the floors were littered with debris. The humid breeze whistled through the numerous holes that dotted the walls through the brick and mortar.

"Rooms had papers strewn about the floor. Some still had the metal bed frames that were rusted. One room we passed had a straitjacket lying on an old tattered spring mattress. It was damp, dirty, and showed clear signs of wear. It gave me the creeps." The doctor nodded in understanding while continuing her note taking.

"My husband was in a room trying for EVPs, so I took the opportunity to snap several photos up and down the hall. If I remember correctly, we were on the third floor. This floor was where many of the criminally insane and psychotic patients were held and so-called 'treated'. There was certainly an eerie feeling the entire time we were there. It was extremely dark; there was no electricity running to the building we were in. The only light came from our flashlights or camera flashes.

"I kept feeling like we were being watched. I looked over my shoulder several times, thinking someone other than my husband was standing there. I even felt someone touch me several times but chalked it up to a breeze or a spider web. Even so, the air felt thick, the feeling was not pleasant, and I fought off running out more than a few times." Laura's eyes shone with a wild spark as she recalled the night.

"An hour had gone by, and we decided to wrap up the evening. We gathered our things and headed to the exit. I stopped before the door and decided to scroll through the photos I had taken. I was stunned at what I saw. The digital screen showed every picture I had snapped had some form of a black shadow in it. One looked like an arm, another like a head, and another looked like a complete body. But then, the last one had multiple shadow figures.

"My heart was pounding, and my entire body started to shake. I tried to tell my husband, who was already at the door, but I couldn't get the words out. I was in a state of shock. I slung the camera around my neck and dashed for my husband and the door. I wanted out of there. That's when it happened." The color drained from Laura's face.

"I took a step forward, and I could see multiple shadow figures quickly moving toward me. I screamed, panicked, and closed my eyes as tight as I could. My husband turned to see why I was screaming, and he saw them as well. I could feel my body being pushed and pulled. I could feel fingers poking me and muffled growls in my ears. I was never so scared in my life. I did everything I could to move but kept getting pulled farther into the building.

"Thankfully, my husband grabbed both of my hands and pulled me to him. I was able to break free, and we escaped as fast as we could. We ran through the door and across the grass. We'd never ran so fast in our lives. Once we reached the car, we started it and drove off the property as quickly as possible. It was an absolute nightmare." Relief poured over Laura's tortured features.

"As if that night wasn't bad enough, a few nights ago, my husband and I were certain we saw a shadow person in our house—maybe more than one. At first, we just thought it was our imaginations or some kind of bad dream, but we're not sure. We are horrified to think that they may have followed us home somehow."

"Well, that is certainly a remarkable story Laura." Dr. Murphy stopped taking notes and set her pen down.

"Laura, you mentioned the name Nancy, correct?"

"Yeah, the horrible nurse." Laura squirmed in her

chair, still twirling her hair.

"Laura, I'd like to show you something." Dr. Murphy retrieves a black and white photo from a manila envelope and hands it to Laura.

"Hmmm, she looks exactly like me," Laura says with a smirk, yet a puzzled look on her face.

"She certainly does. Laura, that is Nancy." Dr. Murphy's face was grave and concerned as she then asked, "You said the shadow people are now in your home?"

"Oh my God!"

VOODOO APP

Rachel grew up in the suburbs of Bedford and obtained her degree from Lynchburg College. Growing up, her parents always told her to never talk to strangers, don't walk down dark alleys, and stay away from bad neighborhoods. Good advice, really. Perhaps another useful piece of advice her parents should have given her was to avoid installing phone apps that had the potential for evil.

On a cool October evening close to midnight, Rachel was meeting friends in downtown Lynchburg on the Bluffwalk for a few drinks and catching up. Rachel had just moved back to town after graduating from college as a research analyst. Not a glamorous career, but she had always been good with delving into topics and numbers, so it seemed a good fit. Her friends, Ella and Chrissie, on the other hand, went on slightly different paths. Chrissie married rich, so continuous shopping took the place of education, and Ella became a real estate agent. All three had been friends since high school and remained in touch over the last four years.

The three met, drank, and shared stories of their latest drama, fun exploits, and their other escapades. The bartender announced last call, so the ladies grabbed one more drink. Rachel wasn't used to drinking so much and was feeling quite tipsy as well as nauseous. She excused herself from the table and headed to the restroom. It only took a minute for her to be on her knees in front of the toilet. She then washed her face in the sink and checked herself in the mirror.

"Hello, beautiful." A tall thin woman with jet black hair was standing behind her.

Rachel hadn't noticed anyone in the restroom when she entered but figured she probably came in while she was face deep in the porcelain pot.

"Are you talking to me?" Rachel looked into the mirror at the mysterious woman.

"Of course, dear, who else would I be speaking to?" The woman chuckled as she placed a cigarette between her bright red lips and lit it.

Rachel washed her hands, trying to ignore the woman. She didn't know her and wasn't feeling up to having any conversation with anyone, let alone a stranger in a seedy bar restroom.

"Trouble with an ex-boyfriend?" The woman took a drag from the cigarette and blew the puff of smoke up to the ceiling.

Rachel looked puzzled. She had no idea who this woman was, and she was, in fact, having trouble with an ex-boyfriend. But how did this stranger know this?

"How do you know that?" Rachel asked with a confused look and a 'none of your business' tone.

"Oh my dear, every girl has troubles with an ex-boyfriend, right?"

Rachel shrugged her shoulders, thinking the statement was true enough. Rachel was tired and clearly not feeling well. She just wanted to leave the bar to go home and sleep. She dried her hands and gave a slight wave goodbye to the woman, turned, and faced the door.

"Rachel, would you like to get some nice, cold revenge on that ex-boyfriend of yours?" The woman asked playfully with a sinister grin.

"Wait, how did you know my name?" Rachel turned to face the stranger.

"Not important, dear. What's important is that you get that boy back for the cheating, the lies, and the heartache he put you through."

Rachel had been in a troublesome three-year relationship with Ben. The first year passed well enough, but the last two years were quite rough. Ben was a classic cheater, a pathological liar, and mentally and physically abusive at times. They had broken up and got back together over a dozen times. Rachel finally broke it off for good five months ago, but Ben still harassed her whenever he could.

"Yeah, he's a giant pain, but what can I do about it?" Rachel stated gloomily, hanging her head down.

"I have just the thing for you, my dear. Let me see your cell phone."

Reluctantly Rachel surrendered her cell phone to the mysterious woman. Her head was pounding, and she just wanted to go home for some Ibuprofen and her warm bed. The woman took Rachel's cell phone, her fingers flying across the screen until she came to a specific app.

"There you go, dear. All set. Have fun." The woman placed the cell phone back in Rachel's hand with a smile, put her cigarette out in the sink, and left the restroom.

Rachel rubbed her head and placed her cell phone in her pocket. She was too tired and nauseous to care what the woman did to her phone. She made her way out into the bar and joined her friends back at the table. The three paid their tabs and left the bar. Ella and Chrissie gave Rachel a ride home. She passed out moments after she stripped off her coat and boots and hit her bed.

Morning came with bright sunshine peeking through Rachel's bedroom blinds. Her head was pounding. She took a few Ibuprofen and sat in a chair, attempting to wake up. Her head felt foggy, and her stomach was still upset. She thought about eating breakfast, but every time she did, her stomach would rumble in a bad way.

Rachel's cell phone rang; Ella was calling to see how she was doing. They had a good but brief conversation.

As Rachel set the phone back down, a notification filled her screen. She looked at her phone, confused. There was a new app on her phone she didn't recognize. The icon was a voodoo doll.

"Voodoo App. What the heck is that?" Rachel said out loud, staring at it, perplexed. She rubbed her eyes and contemplated tapping it. Finally, curiosity got the best of her. She clicked it.

Rachel's eyes widened. Regret immediately filled her mind as she clicked on the app, but it was too late. The app opened, and her screen was filled with a voodoo doll and instructions.

Want sweet cold revenge on someone? You've come to the right app. Simply upload a photo of your victim, then select one or more of the pre-selected pins, or create your own pins, and then drag and drop on the doll's body and then let the fun begin.

A chill ran down Rachel's spine. It scared her at first, but then she thought to herself, *There's no way this is real. No way this thing actually works,* and yet there was some sincere doubt. She vaguely remembered the night before and the mysterious woman in the restroom. She blew everything off as just some random person and random app. She talked herself out of this being a serious thing.

"Okay fine, I'll play along." Rachel said out loud in a playful tone.

She clicked the upload button on the app and found a photo of her ex, Ben. Upload complete.

"Okay, Ben, you idiot, let's have some fun," Rachel smirked and began clicking on pins pulling them to the doll and dropping them. She quickly selected pre-made pins, headache, stubbed toe, stomach ache, and to add a little more sinister pain, blow to the head. She didn't want to kill him, not right now anyway, just wanted him to feel some physical discomfort. She thought the idea of it was fun anyway. After she was satisfied with her pins of choice, she clicked the submit button. The voodoo doll smiled, and that was it. The app closed.

Rachel chuckled at the idea of her ex-boyfriend getting a little jab and perhaps a little pain in the head. She set her phone down and decided to make herself a pot of coffee. She spent the rest of the day watching television and doing everything she could to relieve her hangover. She put herself to bed that night early.

Early the next morning, her cell phone rang. Barely awake, Rachel answered.

"Rachel, are you awake?"

"Ella? Is that you?" Rachel recognized Ella's voice, but there was a tone of excitement.

"Are you watching the news?" Ella asked.

"No, I'm not. I'm not even up yet. Why?" Rachel rubbed her eyes and stretched her arms.

"Get up and turn on the news. Do it. Turn it on. You will not believe it." Ella's enthusiasm was strange to Rachel. She had never heard Ella get so worked up about something.

Rachel found her television remote on the nightstand, clicked, and found the local morning news.

"The subject's body was found in his apartment early this morning. There was no sign of forced entry, and authorities have ruled out suicide. Once again, Benjamin Ellison was found dead. Any information, please contact the local police department."

"Holy crap, your ex is dead! That's crazy! Serves him right for being such a jerk" Ella was rambling on the phone.

Rachel's phone dropped to her pillow. She was frozen with shock.

"No! No! No! It can't be. It's not real. It can't be real." Tears streamed from Rachel's eyes. She was overwhelmed. The feeling hit her right in the heart. The app was real and that she just murdered Ben.

"Oh God... What do I do? What do I do?" Rachel was panicking. She grabbed her phone, clicked the Voodoo App, and tried to uninstall it. It didn't work. She desperately tried to uninstall again and again, but it wouldn't work.

As she stared at her phone, the app opened itself, and the voodoo doll filled the screen. The photo upload portion of the doll's face began to scroll through Rachel's saved photos on its own.

"What is going on? What's happening? God, NO!" Rachel was terrified. She tried to close the app, but it wouldn't close. She tried to power down the phone, but it would not stop.

The upload was complete. The photo this time was of Chrissie. The pins started flying across the screen. One landed on the doll's chest labeled "Elevator". Rachel flipped the app closed and called Chrissie as fast as she could. Her body was shaking, barely able to click on Chrissie's contact page. Her breathing was fast and heavy. She felt like she was going to throw up.

"Chrissie! Chrissie! Where are you? Where are you right now?" Rachel's screamed when she heard Chrissie answer.

"Calm down Rachel, what is with you?" Chrissie replied.

"Chrissie, are you near an elevator? Don't get on the elevator, Chrissie!" Rachel screamed into the phone.

"What? Rachel, you're not making any sense, and why are you yelling?" Chrissie was confused.

"Don't get on the elevator! Don't!" Rachel gripped her cell phone tight, almost cracking it.

"Rachel, what's wrong with the elevator? I'm already on....." the call went dead.

"Chrissie! Chrissie! NO!!" Rachel screamed. Her face was red, veins pulsing out of her neck and forehead.

Rachel dropped the phone. She was crying uncontrollably. And then the phone app opened again, the voodoo doll appeared and began scrolling the saved photos. Rachel frantically tried to delete all of her photos, but the app kept interrupting her. She was able to remove all of her pictures except one. The app unloaded it with a pin labeled "Strangle".

Rachel heard a knock on her door.

"One second." She replied, looking toward the door.

She looked back at the phone. The photo on the voodoo doll was hers.

DEAD DIARY

September 13th, 2020.

My name is Jack Carter, this is my journal, and the world has gone to Hell. There's really no other way to say it. It has gone to Hell. This is not a joke; this is not a made-up story. It's just insane. I'm not sure what to say. They just kept coming and coming. No matter what we did, they never seemed to stop. We had no idea where they came from or how they came to be. It was a nightmare, just like out of a horror movie. But this was happening in real life.

It all happened so fast, and no one saw it coming. They are quick, not like the slow, lethargic ones you see in most of the old zombie movies. No, these things are fast, and some of them are quite sneaky. And if they get a hold of you... Well, it's terrifying. They are like piranhas attacking a dead goat or something. It's a frenzy of teeth and blood.

Yesterday, a week after it all came down; myself, my wife Alisha, and my brother Edward jumped into his truck and safely made it to his house. We stocked the truck as fast as we could with food, blankets, firearms, and ammunition along with an ax and hunting knives. We made our way to our family deer hunting camp near Clair, Michigan, and took up a defensive position. We listened to the radio to find out what was happening out in the rest of the country. The news was horrendous.

October 1st, 2020.

Our camp was overrun a few days ago, forcing us to flee. Six of us made our way down from Michigan to Amherst, Virginia. Word got out to the living that there was a massive compound on the coast near Hampton where people were safe; or as safe as could be. Michigan was overrun within days. Many fled north to take refuge in the thick woods of the Upper Peninsula. Last we had heard there were still a few holding out in make-shift bunkers and prepper type shelters. As for us, we headed south. Getting out of Michigan was difficult. We acquired an SUV for the six of us, but it broke down south of Dundee. We went on foot for days crossing the Ohio border.

Ohio was, for the most part, a ghost-town; no one alive and no one undead. We were able to secure another SUV to drive across southern Ohio and through West Virginia. We took turns driving and sleeping, stopping at abandoned gas stations for food and water. We were all on high alert, not really getting much sleep. In West Virginia, we did encounter two of them while at a gas station. Lucky for us, we spotted them before they were able to attack us. We took them out quickly and left before any more turned up.

We have learned that there seems to be only three things that will stop them. Shooting them. Yeah, shooting them works, but it has to be in the heart or in the head. If you don't hit one or the other, they just keep coming. Stabbing them in the heart or head is the second way that works or basically taking the head right off. Gruesome, I know, but they are relentless killers. The third is fire. They just stand there like they're trying to figure out what is going on. Then their body contorts with bones cracking and snapping. And they scream…my God do they scream. It's a sound you've never heard before all of this and one you'll always remember.

October 10th, 2020.

They're gone! My beautiful Alisha is gone. And my brother. Gone! I can't believe it. It all happened so fast. We were on foot in the woods of Virginia, trying to make it to Hampton. It was dawn; we thought it was safe to move. We hadn't heard anything throughout the night. As we walked past an abandoned market, five of them burst through the door and came running toward us. We raised our weapons as fast as we could, but they closed the distance on us quickly. The market was about 30 yards from us, but these things run so fast. I was able to shoot two, and Ed was able to shoot one, but by the time I was able to aim at a fourth, it was already on top of Ed. His gun went flying into the air, and the zombie ripped into his neck. There was so much blood.

One of the guys traveling with us was able to kill the fifth one and then turned his sights on the fourth one, but it was too late. Ed was gone. I looked at Ed lying there motionless. I walked over to him, but I knew there was no saving him. I looked at my wife. She was standing there crying. We heard movement toward the back of the store; two more were running towards us.

I raised my gun and pulled the trigger twice as fast as I could. Nothing. I was out of ammunition. I frantically tried to reload. My heart was pounding, and my palms were sweating. The other guy fired and was able to hit one. As I raised my gun to fire on the second... it leaped in the air and tackled Alisha. I screamed and ran toward them. I didn't dare fire because I was afraid of hitting my wife. She tried to push the thing off of her. It held her to the ground and sunk its teeth into her neck. As I reached them, I kicked the zombie off of her. Blood spattered all over me. It fought and struggled to finish her. I struck it multiple times in the head with the butt of my gun. I reached to my belt with my left hand, gripped my knife, and then plunged it into its head. Once it slumped down, I kicked it off of me. I crawled to Alisha, but she wasn't breathing.

October 30th, 2020.

This insane situation; it's ironic. Halloween is

tomorrow. It used to be my favorite holiday until now. I remember as a kid, not that long ago really, that my friends and I dressed up like zombies for Halloween. We didn't go trick-or-treating, although we did knock on a few doors and scored a few candy bars. I think I was 14, and Ed was 12, just about to turn 13. We both loved Halloween so much. The year before our zombie outfits, we were medieval knights, ready to save the cute damsels in distress throughout the neighborhood. Those were fun times. I'd give anything to be 14 again, before all of this.

I'm holed up in an abandoned county jail. I'm on the roof with a rifle and binoculars. I don't remember where either came from, but somehow I ended up with them. My head is throbbing in pain. I can't find any Ibuprofen anywhere in this town. There are a few of us here. Strangers really. No one seems to care to get to know each other. Suits me fine. I'm so tired. I haven't slept in weeks.

October 31st, 2020.

I can hear them. They are everywhere. I can hear them running, grunting and growling. I don't know why, but they don't try to get in. They just either run around the building and up and down the streets, or they stand in place, swaying staring up at the sky. I don't take random shots at them, and I've told others not to do it either. I've noticed that if one or two get hit, others nearby become agitated and go crazy. It's best to keep them calm if possible.

I think about my wife and my brother a lot. I have no idea if my other friends and family made it out. I doubt it. I've seen very few survivors. Whatever this is spread so fast and those that got it infected others with just a simple bite or scratch. Life now is exhausting.

November 1st, 2020.

I just can't take it anymore. My will to survive in this new world is gone. I cannot live my life on the run, hiding, fighting, killing, the same thing every day. I've locked myself in one of the old jail cells. I don't want to hurt the others. This will no doubt be my last entry. I let one of them bite me about a half-hour ago. It's just a matter of time before I turn into one of them. Hopefully, someday when the zombies are gone and perhaps when humanity is restored, someone will find this journal. Someone will read it and know what happened.

BOYS BEWARE

BREAKING NEWS: A fire has ravaged a downtown Amherst business overnight. The fire department responded to a fire at The Black Cat Curiosities and Oddities store at approximately 3:00 am this morning. Firefighters found the entire building engulfed in flames. No injuries were reported. Arson is suspected, but no suspects have been arrested.

Billy, Bailey, and Brad Brockton, otherwise known as the Brockton Boys; three brothers who many believe were born lawbreakers. Billy was the oldest at 28 years old, Bailey 26, and Brad 24; they were handsome boys with an affinity for the local ladies and an appetite for immoral and wicked activity. Since birth, they have been in some form of trouble, creating fear and havoc in their town of Amherst, Virginia. Their parents were hard-working, respectable residents who mysteriously died ten years ago. Most of the townsfolk believed the boys had something to do with their death, but nothing could be proven.

The Brockton Boys didn't care whose life they made miserable. They picked on kids, adults, and animals alike. Those who tried to stand up to the boys always met a disastrous fate, severely injured or dead. Even the local police officers were afraid of them. They knew the boys were involved in multiple criminal activities but steered clear of them for fear of what may happen. The boys ran the town, and they knew it.

A few months ago, a new store opened downtown by a newcomer to Amherst. The Black Cat Curiosities and Oddities store opened where an old Five and Dime once flourished. Inside was packed with books on the paranormal, witchcraft, myths and legends as well as herbs, sages, and all things needed for incantations, prayers, and spells. The owner, Fiona, was a beautiful woman in her early 40's who was thin and tall at six-foot. She had long wavy black hair that shimmered. And was a self-proclaimed practicing witch.

Fiona's business was slow to start but eventually had

quite a few people walking through her doors, some for specific reasons, others out of curiosity. She was extremely friendly to the townsfolk and quickly gained a reputable standing within the community. She was even asked to be the Grand Marshall leading the Amherst Halloween parade her first year after opening the store. She happily accepted.

On Halloween morning, Fiona got a call that no business owner wants to receive. The fire department notified her that her business had burned and was a total loss. She was devastated. She had insurance, but the shop contained items that no amount of money could ever replace. Her good nature took a back seat to revenge, and she was determined to find out who set the fire and make them pay.

It wasn't difficult to figure out who the arsonist was... or *arsonists* were. The Brockton Boys had set fires to things all over the county before, and it was no secret that they had given Fiona a hard time. A close friend told Fiona that it was indeed the Brockton Boys. They had been drinking all night, smashing beer bottles all over town, and busting mailboxes. A few witnesses saw them breaking the windows to the Black Cat Curiosities and Oddities, laughing and carrying on like animals. It was only a half-hour later that the entire building was on fire.

Upon hearing the news, Fiona was fuming. She drove around town looking for them, eventually locating their truck parked at the local dive bar. Pulling her black hair back in a ponytail, she composed herself before taking a deep breath and flinging open the door. Everyone in the bar turned to look at who walked through the door.

"Well, well, well, if it isn't the wicked witch." Laughed Billy. The other boys joined in sneering and mocking her. All three were sitting at the bar, turning on their stools to face Fiona.

"What do you want, witch?" Brad asked as he took a long swig of beer.

"Maybe she came to have a drink with us, boys." Bailey smiled and snorted, raising a glass to the air.

Fiona stood in front of them. She was not impressed by their conduct and found them to be downright appalling. She showed no fear and was not about to back down.

"Did you burn down my store?" She asked with a stern

tone, looking all three in the eyes.

Billy got up from the stool and walked toward her with his beer in hand. She stood still. He walked around her and leaned in, an inch from her left ear. She almost gagged from the smell of cigarettes and stale beer wafting from his mouth.

"And what if we did, witch? What are you gonna do about it?" Billy whispered in a condescending voice. His brothers just laughed.

Billy walked around to the other side of Fiona and leaned in toward her right ear. She stood still.

"It's just too bad you weren't in it when we did." Billy walked away, snickering before guzzling his beer. He slammed the empty beer bottle on the bar and yelled to the bartender for another round.

Fiona didn't say a word at the moment. She just turned and walked to the door. As she reached for the door handle, she stopped and turned her head back toward the boys and only said three words.

"Ribbit ribbit, boys," she pushed the door open and left the bar smiling.

The boys looked confused and then started laughing,

thinking she was out of her mind. They grabbed their bottles and continued drinking.

Halloween night came, along with hundreds of children trick-or-treating. Fiona skipped the parade earlier. Instead, she stayed home, flipping through her many spellbooks looking for a specific incantation for hours. She was never into black magic or casting evil spells on anyone in the past. However, she was going to make an exception for the Brockton Boys. And then she found it, the spell she was looking for. She prepared herself and read aloud.

The black shall bring fright on this Halloween night. As the doors open for the dead, the moon shall turn red. Read aloud the damned that shall be and then wait for you shall see. For those that are owed shall forever be a toad.

Fiona finished her ritual, smiled, and headed out into town to enjoy the night's festivities. Although she had missed the parade, she was still able to enjoy the Halloween festival that was held afterward. When she arrived downtown, she was surprised to find many of the townsfolk helping to clean up the burnt pieces from her shop. They were banding together to help her rebuild. A few tears welled up in her eyes as she thanked everyone and joined in.

Three residents were expectedly absent from assisting with Fiona's shop. The Brockton Boys headed to the swamp for some night fishing after a full night of harassing kids and stealing candy. Just about every other night, the boys went into the Virginia swamps to fish for catfish and anything else they could catch. Their cooler was packed with beer and pockets stuffed with cigarettes. They were already drunk before getting into their flat-bottom boat.

An hour or so had passed. The boys had a dozen catfish on the boat flopping around a few dozen empty beer cans. They were laughing and joking around about what they had done to the witch. Their laughter was soon interrupted by the night sky filled with Fiona's laugh. The boys stopped, looked around, confusion plain on their faces.

"What was that?" Billy asked nervously. He seemed to have sobered up quite quickly.

"It was nothing, man. Nothing at all." Brad stated, trying to sound confident, but the stammering and shakiness in his voice took the starch out of his words.

"Yeah, man. Nothing." Bailey was following his brother's lead, even though he heard it as well.

The boys all took a drink from their beer and muttered under their breath. They cast their lines out again but sat in silence. They all looked tense and anxious. Their eyes darted back and forth, up and down. Then, they heard the laugh again accompanied by hundreds of frogs and toads all croaking together.

"There it is again!" Billy jumped up from his boat seat, dropped his fishing pole to the bottom of the boat, and spun his head, trying to find where the sounds were coming from.

All three brothers were on their feet in an instant with their poles on the boat's bottom. They began to sweat, and panic filled their faces.

"My chest, it hurts, my stomach, ah my..." Billy was bent over, holding his stomach. He grimaced in pain. He grunted and groaned as he fell to the floor of the boat.

"My...my...stomach!" Bailey and Brad began to yell in pain, and both fell to the floor.

The Brockton Boys were curled up in the fetal position on the floor of the boat. They began kicking and flailing their feet and hands. They moaned and screamed in agony for over a minute. Then, all fell silent briefly.

"Ribbit! Ribbit!" The sounds of croaking toads arose from the boat.

The bottom of the boat no longer held the three notorious Brockton Boys, but instead three oversized toads with horror on their bumpy brown toad faces. They looked at each other in complete disbelief, hearing Fiona's laugh wafting through the swamp air again. Within minutes, the trees above them filled with screech owls. A screech owl's favorite meals were frogs and toads.

SOUL OF CROW

Josh and I walk out of the coffee shop, enjoying our hot coffee and the warmth of the morning sun on a chilly November morning. We aren't able to get together every morning for coffee, but it is nice when we can. The sky was clear, only a few clouds drifted by. I strain my neck to look up when I hear the *caws*. Crows, as black as night, fly overhead across town, heading toward the cemetery.

"Hey Josh, look at that." I point to the crows above us.

Josh looks up and stares for a moment. "Creepy," he says, taking a sip from his coffee.

As I start to say something else, who happens to drive by at that very moment, but old Rich Coulson himself. A chill runs down my spine, and a quick shiver shakes my body. My coffee sloshes around in the cup, but luckily doesn't spill.

"Josh, do you know why the crows are flying to the old cemetery?"

"No idea, but something tells me you do."

 Josh was smug, acting like a group of crows flying overhead was no big deal, which most of the time, it wasn't, except here in Timberlake.

"Take a look at that old truck driving through town." I point to Rich's truck driving by.

"Yeah, so. What's that got to do with the crows, Peter?"

"Well, let me tell you."

"In that old rusted out truck is Rich Coulson and his old hound Rex. I swear that old truck of his is as old as he is. He probably bought it when he was just ten years old. It's got so much rust on it; I'm not sure what color it is. Rich probably doesn't remember either.

"And along with rust, there's an abundance of dog slobber. Rex drools more than any dog I've ever seen. Come to think of it, Rex is probably as old as the truck. Well, perhaps not, but funny to think about. All three of them have wrinkles and a bit of rust. They must be driving through town to get their morning coffee and donut, then off to the cemetery. It's morning ritual." I tell Josh as we slowly walk down the sidewalk, keeping my eyes fixed on Rich's truck.

"Rich is the caretaker and the creepy gravedigger of the town cemetery and has been since before I was born. From what I know, he was married once but had no children. His wife died from cancer about twenty-five years ago and was laid to rest in the cemetery. Perhaps it's comforting to Rich being able to visit his wife each day. Many people have said he often talks to her while toiling there. Rex usually follows him close behind or naps in the grass or leaf piles in the fall months.

"He's not a big man, about five foot five and I'd say one hundred and forty pounds, but he has a hell of a beard and mustache, doesn't he? It goes down to the middle of his chest and completely covers his face. You can't even see his mouth unless he's stuffing it with a donut. To me, he looks like a cross between a farmer and a lumberjack; he always wears blue jean overalls with a flannel shirt and an old tattered twenties style newsy cap. He's friendly enough. I've never really talked to him, but I usually see him driving around town. If you wave to him, he will wave back." I pause my history lesson and let Josh take it all in.

"Do you want to hear the crazy story about him?"

"Well, you've told me a bunch of stuff so far, so why not." Josh rolls his eyes and swigs more of his coffee.

"Okay, great. So, I had heard that back on a cold and wet November, the night after his wife's funeral and burial, Rich snuck into the cemetery and dug up her body."

"Gross!" Josh scrunched up his face like he just tasted the worst food in the world.

"Indeed, but that's not the worst of it. The story goes that he dug her up because he had some kind of belief that if he surrendered her body to the crows to feed on, then her soul would be saved, and she would come back as a crow herself. He thought that if she were a crow that she would always be around for him to visit."

"What? That is so messed up."

"Yes, it is. Now, that's not all. People have also said that over the years, Rich has dug up dozens of bodies to feed the crows to save their souls."

"What?" Josh's face contorted in disgust.

"Yeah, people say every time the crows fly over town, that means Rich has dug up another body to feed them. It could just be a local legend or rumors, of course, but it wouldn't surprise me if it were true. I mean, why else would those crows gather like that?"

"Okay, wait, so if he's digging up bodies, why hasn't he been arrested?" Josh stops us in our tracks.

"Not enough evidence to hold or convict him. Everyone has suspicions, of course, and most think he certainly did it, but no one has *seen* him do it. Cops have investigated a few times, but they've never found anything. Of course, they've never dug any of the graves either to see if the caskets are empty. Gruesome job, I wouldn't want to do it either. But we all see them though, we all see the crows flying over the town, circling and staying around the cemetery."

"You want to go check it out tonight?" I look at Josh and smile, nodding my head.

"You mean, watch that guy dig up a body?" Josh points toward the cemetery.

"Well, the crows are already flying there, so I bet he's already done it, but we can go see if it's true. See if the crows are feeding."

"Yeah, I don't know, man. Seems kind of crazy." Josh was shaking his head no.

I just stare at him, waiting. I knew I didn't have to say anything, just stare at him and he'll say yes.

"Okay fine, I'll go. Man, I hate this." Josh walks away.

"See you tonight, buddy. Bring a flashlight." I say, smiling as I walk away and head to work.

Night comes; the temperature considerably warm for late fall. A slight breeze comes in from the west, blowing the colorful leaves off of the trees. The moon is nearly full, lots of moonlight peeking through oncoming rain clouds. It hasn't rained yet, but you can smell it in the air.

Josh meets me at the entrance of the cemetery, with flashlights in hand. Josh seems visibly nervous. I'm ecstatic and ready to investigate. The cemetery entrance has massive pillars on each side made of stone and concrete. There once was a wrought iron gate, but there are only portions of it left.

"Hey Josh, you ready?" I ask, knowing he's a little freaked out.

"Yeah, Peter, sure, let's do this." Josh's voice shuddered, and I could hear the apprehension.

"It'll be fun man, trust me."

"Fun? Seeing big, black birds eating dead bodies… That's fun for you?" Josh stopped walking and looks at me with contention.

"Well…okay, not fun, but… Let's just go." I walk down the path and wave him on.

We walk a gravel path about fifty yards, winding through thick hedgerows and trees that eventually lead to the tombstones and graves. I can hear the crows cawing getting louder the farther we walk. Josh and I walk as quietly as we can and use our flashlights only when we need to. As we approach a grouping of trees, we hear a voice. It was Rich, talking to his dog, Rex.

We crouch down behind a bush and lift our heads to see. Twenty feet from us, near a massive oak tree, Rich and Rex stood near a large wooden wagon with a lit lantern. Dozens and dozens of crows fill the oak tree above them. Every branch is full of the black birds. The caws are nearly deafening. As a light rain begins to come down, Rich tips the wagon and out slides a freshly dug up dead body. The caws get louder.

"Holy crap!" Josh whispers and slaps me on the shoulder.

"Oh man, I told you! I told you. I *knew* it was true."

Rex jumps up on the now empty wagon and sits. He looks up at the crows and watches. Rich pulls the wagon away from the body and then joins his dog sitting on the wagon. He takes an apple from his overall pocket for a snack. As soon as he bites down, the crows descend from the oak branches. The frenzy of black feathers and beaks is raucous and madness. It only takes them mere seconds to strip the body of clothes and tear into flesh. Josh and I were stunned at the horrific scene.

"This is sick man. I don't like this; I gotta get out of here." Josh says, visibly shaking.

"I agree; this is worse than I thought."

We crept away from the bush to make our way back to

the path. When we reached the gravel path, I took one last look at the gruesome scene. The crows are loud with their constant caws and devouring of the body. Even though the light rain and casual breeze rustle the leaves, we can hear bones cracking and the corpse being torn apart. As we take a last look, Rich turns his head toward us, clearly interlopers. He points his old finger at us and states in an ominous tone, "The crows will feed on you soon."

We ran down the path, never looking back. We jump into our cars and both speed away as fast as we can.

Days go by; Josh and I didn't speak to each other about what happened. We have silently decided to ignore it. We hear a caw from above, then another and another as we stad on the sidewalk outside of the coffee shop, enjoying our coffees. Josh and I both look up to see all of the buildings in town were lined with crows. Hundreds of them, all looking down at us.

STRAWMAN

Adam stood at the edge of the cornfield alone. He had a flashlight and nothing else; no firearm, no weapon of any kind. It's the first time Adam had gone near a cornfield, let alone entered one in twenty-five years. The last time he saw his father, Mark, was when he was five years old. His father went into the cornfield, the very same cornfield, and never came out. Rumors abound that his father's disappearance was everything from being swallowed up by an underground sinkhole, alien abduction, and kidnapped by Bigfoot to just walking away from his life and family to start a new one somewhere else. Growing up, none of the stories and facets of gossip were plausible in Adam's mind because he knew the truth. He tried telling his mother, his grandfather, and anyone else who would stand still long enough, and although they listened, they didn't believe him. No one believed a five-year-old boy. "The Strawman," he would say. "The Strawman."

It was around midnight when Adam entered the cornfield in late October with a heavy mist and patches of rain. The Virginia sky was full of stars and a full moon; a harvest moon or blood moon as many call it. It was bright, but a dark orange hue tinged the entire circumference. A few clouds peppered the dark sky passing over the orange moon, hindering the glow every so often. The air was blustery and chilly enough that Adam could see his breath. He wore a thick sweatshirt, wool cap, and gloves to keep the bitter air at bay.

Cornstalks filled acres and acres of farmland. They spilled over the horizon, stopping only at the trees in the far background. The cornstalks were dry, devoid of the vibrant summer-like green coloring. They were dull, tanned by the sun, dirty and crumbling. The sound of the stalks swaying back and forth created a harsh rustling. The unpleasant odors of dirt and manure mixed with decay and rain made a God awful stench that singed Adam's nose, even standing just at the edge.

It wasn't just the eerie scene, of course. Knowing his

father's demise in this very cornfield twenty-five years ago to the day also had Adam on edge. However, Adam felt it was his destiny to return. For years he fought himself; the inner demons of guilt for not saving his father then, but of course he was just a child, what could he have done and the deep-seated craving for revenge, to avenge his father by eliminating what took him. Either way, he still holds blame and guilt close to his heart and deep in his mind. He believed that if he could find it and kill it, no one else would disappear, thus making him a hero to the town. And by destroying it, it may provide a slice of peace he hasn't had since childhood.

The town Concord, Virginia, had a decline in population since the 1940s. Some people moved out on their own, some were victims of criminal activities, and some were casualties of accidents. And many, the many most people don't want to talk about, have just simply disappeared. Since Mark vanished, there have been forty-five cases of missing people. Many of their photos are still hanging on bulletin boards throughout the town.

Adam, of course, knew that the missing people of Concord most likely fell victim to the Strawman. This thing was smart, cunning, and inconspicuous. Hundreds of people drove by it without ever giving it a second thought, like any other scarecrow out there, unassuming and dull. Just about every cornfield and garden in the country had some form of a scarecrow. Ironic really, because scarecrows never seem to scare a crow away, in fact just the opposite. Many crows and ravens have been seen perching on the arms and heads of scarecrows for years.

The truth was Adam wanted to avenge his father for years but felt he wasn't physically or mentally ready. He drove by the cornfield several times and even stopped and stood on the edge of the field once. He knew he would have to do it alone but didn't have a clue how to destroy it. He spent years researching the occult, paranormal science, demonology, religion, and anything else he thought would help give him the tools to defeat it. He spoke with religious leaders, paranormal investigators, and interviewed anyone with similar stories. Never a big religious person when he was younger, but Adam's faith grew the more studying he did. He prayed every night for the strength and wisdom, and he felt it didn't hurt to always carry a rosary, a crucifix, the Star of David, and even a four-leaf clover.

As Adam stood at the edge of the cornfield, his mind flashed back to October 1995. It was as if his adult self was standing right behind his five-year-old self. He could see his father again, waving to him from the combine. It was bright red, enormous, and loud. It cut rows and rows of corn like it was nothing. Mark would wave to Adam every pass of a row, and Adam waved back with a big smile. He loved his father and saw him as the biggest strongest man in the world, especially when he was driving the massive combine.

That day, as Mark and the combine mowed down the cornstalks, Adam was distracted for a moment. He stared at the scarecrow in the middle of the field. It was mounted high above the stalks, dressed in blue jeans and boots with straw poking out the bottoms and a ragged, red flannel shirt covered the torso with the straw sticking out the armholes. Its face was dirty burlap, and a dark brown leather hat adorned its head.

He was distracted because he swore it had moved. Five-year-olds have vivid imaginations to be sure, but he honestly did see it move. He looked at the combine and then looked back at the scarecrow. It moved *again*. The combine rolled past it. Mark waved to

Adam. Adam waved back with a smile, and then looked back at the scarecrow. It was gone!

Adam's smile disappeared in an instant, and his face filled with terror. He looked back at the combine, but his father was no longer in the cab. Mark was being held up in the air by the Strawman. The scarecrow's straw feet were planted on the roof of the cab. His arms stretched out, holding Mark upside down by his feet. Mark was screaming and swinging his arms wildly. Adam was frozen in fear. The Strawman turned his dirty, tattered burlap sack face toward Adam, showing a sinister smile. The combine continued to move, churning stalks and spitting out dry withered corn. The Strawman let out a howl and released his grip on Mark's feet. Adam's father fell headfirst into the whipping combine blades as Adam watched.

Adam snapped out of his mind's flashback as tears flowed down his cheeks. He missed his father. His moment of sadness quickly changed to anger and the thought of payback. At that moment, on the edge of the cornfield, he heard the howl. He was scared, no doubt, but he was ready. He reached into his shirt pocket, grasping and rubbing his rosary and crucifix. He then looked up at the sky and screamed as loud as he could.

"STRAWMAN!! I'M COMING FOR YOU!!!"

Adam entered the cornfield and quickly moved down the row toward the middle of the field. His flashlight helped to show the way, but at that moment, he was running on adrenaline. The closer to the middle of the field he got, he could hear the howls getting louder. The Strawman was not attempting to flee or hide, likely considering Adam as just another person to go missing, more prey.

Adam reached the middle of the field. There was a twenty-five-foot circumference devoid of any cornstalks. In the center was a long, thick wooden pole. Attached to the pole was the Strawman. Adam stopped and looked up at it, and the Strawman looked down at Adam. The burlap face stretched wide in a menacing grin. His eyeless holes squinted as he raised a straw hand and gripped the brim of his leather hat. He tugged slightly on the brim and nodded his head, gesturing "hello" to Adam.

Adam looked up at it and began to pray aloud, tossing out scripture. Within a second, the Strawman jumped off of his wooden perch and onto the muddy ground.

He looked Adam in the eye and began to laugh. The laugh was evil and threatening. The two danced around each other, staring and moving closer to each other with every circle. Adam said nothing, but the Strawman kept up his sinister laugh.

The Strawman leaped into the air hitting Adam square in the face, and Adam fell to the ground gasping for air. The Strawman grabbed Adam's leg pulling him from the dirt and tossed him around. His strength caught Adam off guard. He had no idea it would be so strong. Adam continued to get thrown and punched. Blood was dripping from his nose and his mouth, and he had cuts and bruises beginning to appear all over his body. He wasn't going to last much longer.

As Adam lie on the mud-covered ground, he was able to reach into his front pants pocket. He pulled out a metal flask. As the Strawman stood over him, he poured the contents over its frayed jeans and boots. It was filled with fuel that a priest had blessed. Not your average holy water, but he knew - he hoped - that fire would incinerate it, and the blessing would destroy it for good. Adam reached into his other pocket to retrieve a Zippo lighter. The Strawman leaned down with his face an inch from Adam's.

With a soulless scratchy voice, the Strawman finally spoke. "Time to die, boy."

Adam gripped the lighter and winked at the scarecrow towering over him as the Strawman reached for Adam's throat, the lighter sparked and flashed with fire. In a split second, the Strawman's lower half was overcome with flames. Adam scrambled out from underneath its legs, pushing himself backward across the muck. It didn't take long for the Strawman to be consumed entirely in fire.

At first, the Strawman let out a howl and a menacing laugh. He looked down at Adam and yelled, "Nice try, boy!"

Adam's expression turned to confusion and apprehension. The priest was certain that blessing the fuel would undoubtedly send the scarecrow back to whatever Hell he came from. The Strawman, engulfed in the fire, took a step toward Adam. Adam scrambled backward, trying to get to his feet. He knew he had no other weapons and no other means to defeat it.

Once the fire reached the scarecrow's head, the Strawman stopped. It began to scream and howl louder than ever. It thrashed its straw body and flailed its arms wildly. Adam knew something was happening. It was working. He sprang to his feet, grabbed the crucifix, rosary, Star of David, and even the four-leaf clover out of his shirt pocket. He rubbed them and then pointed them at the Strawman. He shouted prayers and demanded that it be sent to Hell.

Adam was out of breath, his heart pounded, and sweat dripped off of his beaten body. He was shaking, causing everything in his hands to rattle. He watched in satisfaction as the Strawman disintegrated into a cloud of fine dust on the ground. The howls dissipated and were finally silenced. Adam collapsed to the ground and tried to catch his breath. It was over. After all these years, it was over.

Adam lifted himself off of the ground, brushed off the grime, trying to ignore the pain he was in. He limped through the field, back to his vehicle. He looked up at the sky, said one final prayer, and said thank you to his late father. Adam looked back one last time at the peaceful cornfield and drove away.

The chilly air continued to gust through the cornfield. It was quiet, aside from the cornstalks swaying back and forth. The breeze wafted over the pile of ash, picked it up and carried it through the air. Its particles latched on to a few of the cornstalks. Rays of orange moonlight flickered upon them. They began to move.

LEGEND OF VIRGINIA TRAIN 403

I'll tell you a story about a cute couple I met one afternoon in the park—a couple looking for adventure. Quinn and Lexi were from Fort Hill, Virginia. They were high school sweethearts that got married right after graduation. They attended the same college; they got the same degrees and even worked for the same company. They were made for each other. Soulmates, as they say.

Now, I didn't know them long, only about a month. They had a dog, as did I, and we met at a dog park back in September. Our dogs actually met first and ran off together. We had to track them down and separate them. Cute really, and that led to dinner and drinks later that night and a kind of quick friendship. They were very nice, itching for some tremendous journey, and lucky for them, I was able to give it to them.

I wasn't a travel agent or even some kind of tourism advocate, but I have logged plenty of travel miles in my years on the roads, trains, and through the air. I loved all of my trips; for the most part, all had good and bad times. I would have to say that my travels by train were some of my favorites, and to be honest, I didn't always ride with a paid ticket.

Jumping onto a freight train and stowing away in the empty cars can be an exhilarating shot of adrenalin. The freedom to come and go as you please, the mystery, the places to see and experience, and of course, not cost a dime. I have been able to go coast to coast, experiencing all of the great things each state has to offer. Now, of course, as with any type of exploration and venture, there are always the possibilities of inherent risks.

Riding the rails without a ticket and stowing away on freight trains encompasses a lot of dangerous situations and a real threat of peril. You become vulnerable to severe weather at times, unscheduled stops, car searches, hobos who certainly don't like strangers on their turf, and other things that I'll just call paranormal.

Well, anyway, Lexi and Quinn were quite the daring and carefree couple, and they were looking for something to do. They had vacation time coming up, and I thought I would help them out. I told them about my previous exploits, specifically my train trips. Their eyes got wide, and faces filled with enthusiasm as I gabbed. It was only about three weeks later, and they had made up their mind.

On a crisp October day, Lexi and Quinn packed two backpacks with water, change of clothes, blankets, and snacks, and once the sun had set, they made the trek to the Norfolk Southern Railway System rail yard. They were excited to be on this new voyage together. They had their sights set on the 45 car Virginia freight train 403.

The two waited for the sky to go dark, the railroad company to change crews, do their initial inspection, and then ran as fast as they could for an empty rail car. Quinn jumped on and helped Lexi board. The two quietly celebrated for making it without being seen, made their way to the back of the car, and made themselves comfortable.

The rail car was empty, aside from the dirt and dust layer on the timeworn wooden floor. The wooden slats on the walls weren't exactly straight and let in rays of the full moon's light. The large door was slightly open, hanging from rusted iron tracks. The smell was somewhat musty and dank. Lexi and Quinn didn't care, though; they were thrilled to be there.

An hour or so had passed. It was close to 11:00 pm. The temperature dropped, and light rain started to tap the metal roof of the rail car. The couple broke out their blankets and used them for something soft to sit on. They settled in as the train began to move and leave the yard. They were on their way. They didn't exactly know where they were going, and to them, that was the best part of their trip.

The trained rolled down the tracks quickly. The couple pushed open the large door enough to sit on the edge with their feet dangling out. They embraced and enjoyed the cool wind and the nighttime sights and lights passing by. They never felt so free and energized and a little nervous. They had never done anything quite like this before.

Midnight came, and Lexi was tired. They laid out a blanket to sleep on and one to cover up with. The movement of the train, the breeze, and the sounds of the clacking had them both asleep within minutes. They were miles away from home and at the whim of wherever the train was taking them.

"Quinn? Quinn, wake up." Lexi shook Quinn's arm.

"Huh, what? What is it, Lexi?"

"I hear something. Someone is in the car with us." She whispered in his ear.

"What? No, that's impossible. We've been moving this whole time. No one was in this car when we got on." Quinn whispered back.

"Quinn, listen, I can hear breathing." Lexi's voice was shaky and cracking. Quinn could sense the fear in her. He'd never heard panic like that in her voice before.

Quinn lifted his head about an inch, cocking his right ear toward the middle of the train car. He looked around the car but heard and saw nothing. He slowly removed the blanket from them and dug around in his backpack for a flashlight. He tried to be as quiet as possible. The only thing he could hear over the train noise was Lexi's heart pounding and his own. The train was still moving quickly. Only flecks of light penetrated the slats in the wood.

Quinn continued listening for anything other than him or Lexi. He found the small flashlight in his pack and shined it toward the other end of the train car. Lexi was holding onto his arm as tightly as she could. She was shaking. Quinn's flashlight scanned the far end of the car, back and forth. Nothing. He shined it to the left and right of them. Nothing.

"There's nothing here, Lexi. The car is empty, just you and me." Quinn turned the light off and rubbed Lexi's head.

"Are you sure? I swear, I heard something." Lexi still held onto Quinn's arm tight; her eyes darted all over the space.

"You saw, I shined the light all over and..." Quinn abruptly stopped talking. He could hear breathing. But it wasn't Lexi or himself. It was deep, dark, concentrated.

"You hear it, don't you?" Lexi squeezed Quinn's arm so tight he winced.

Quinn turned the flashlight on again and scanned every inch of the car slowly. Nothing. Then they heard the breathing, louder, followed by a growl. It was a drawn-out guttural growl. Quinn and Lexi's throats tightened, both swallowed hard. They knew something was in the car and it wasn't human.

The growl came again. Quinn's arm raced with the flashlight shining everywhere, and then he pointed it above them. Quinn's eyes practically bulged out of his head. His heart pounded, and he blew out a breath as if the wind had been knocked out of him. He immediately had tears pouring from his eyes.

"Lexi... Dear God... Lexi. It's above us." Quinn

stuttered, barely able to get the words out.

Lexi tilted her head up, but with eyes closed. She could feel Quinn's body tensing and shaking. She wanted to look but didn't want to look. Her body began to tremble, matching Quinn's. She started to cry without even knowing why. What was above them growled again and inched its way down the wall toward them. Lexi could hear claws scrapping the wood behind them. She opened her eyes.

Clutching the ceiling, the back wall, and the sidewall was an enormous creature. It was unlike anything the couple had ever seen before. It had six arms with claws dug into the train car wood. Its body was an intense dark purple, shaped like a human-sized spider. Its face looked almost human but was demon-like with horns and two soulless black eyes. Quinn's flashlight bounced off of its eyes as Quinn shook.

The creature moved slowly toward them, growling and snarling as its face contorted, revealing its massive teeth. Quinn and Lexi were frozen with fear as one arm reached toward Lexi's face and stopped just short of touching her. They tried to move, but neither could.

The creature's claw lightly touched Lexi's face, then harder, piercing the skin and slowly tearing it. Lexi let out a scream.

The creature moved its claw away; its face grimaced and let out an ear-piercing howl that deafened the terrified couple. The creature released its grip from the ceiling and walls crashing down right on top of them. The beast flailed its arms, its claws ripping and teeth tearing. The screams could be heard through the breeze as Virginia train 403 continued down the tracks. Blood dripped through the floorboards from one town to the next.

Well, it's a gruesome story, I know. It's a shame Quinn and Lexi had to meet their fate that way. I liked those two, I really did. How do I know all this? Who do you think gave Lexi and Quinn the idea and told them which train to ride? Who do you think was there? I feel bad, but I mean, someone has to feed that thing.

Thank you so much for purchasing this book and helping to support Hill City Paranormal, Wicked Harvest Books and all the great adventures and more books to come. We sincerely hope you enjoy the stories, and you will share them with family and friends. We also hope you'll visit our websites and multiple social media pages and share these with friends and family as well.

Have fun and join us in exploring the world of all things paranormal...and the beyond!

TALES FROM THE BEYOND – Series One

Haunted History Tours - Academy Center of the Arts 2019

TALES FROM THE BEYOND – Series One

Medoc State Park, Littleton Bigfoot Investigation

TALES FROM THE BEYOND – Series One

Staton Investigation Behind The Scenes

TALES FROM THE BEYOND – Series One

FRANKIE B. BIGFOOT

TALES FROM THE BEYOND – Series One

WOODY G. WATTS

and

HILL CITY PARANORMAL

Website – www.HillCityParanormal.com

Social Media – @hillcityparanormal

Podcast – Hill City Paranormal

Call Us – 701-HAUNTED

Email – hillcityparanormal@gmail.com

JERROD S. SMELKER

and

WICKED HARVEST BOOKS

www.WickedHarvestBooks.com

www.JerrodSmelker.com

www.LastLeafPublishing.com

Instagram – authorsmelker

Facebook – Wicked Harvest Books

Blog – Spooky Stories MI -
https://spookystoriesmi.blogspot.com/

Blog – The Smelker Files -
https://smelkerfiles.blogspot.com/

Contact – jsmelker@hotmail.com

Other Published Books and Stories by author
Jerrod S. Smelker
Available at Amazon.com and select bookstores

- Wicked Harvest: Michigan Monsters and Macabre – Series One
  - o Paperback and eBook
- Vigilant in Today's World: Volume 1
  - o Paperback and eBook
- Amusing Anecdotes from Boot Camp
  - o Paperback and eBook
- Lies in the Attic – Short Story eBook
- Casey – Short Story eBook
- "Welcome to the Neighborhood" featured in GLAHW's Ghostlight - Spring 2019
- "The Abandoned" featured in GLAHW's Erie Tales 11: Tales from the Asylum

  - o Soon to be Published:
    - Nina
    - Orphan King
    - Killer Karma
    - Heaven's Heroes
    - Wicked Harvest: Michigan Monsters & Macabre - Series Two

TALES FROM THE BEYOND – Series One

TALES FROM THE BEYOND – Series One

Made in the USA
Monee, IL
25 April 2025